AMONG *Us*

Among Us

Zane Michaels

Published in 2022 by Zone 4 Kidz
An imprint of Tamarind Hill Press Limited

ISBN Paperback: 978-1-915161-96-3
ISBN eBook: 978-1-915161-95-6

Tamarind Hill Press Limited
Copies are available at special rates for bulk orders. Contact us on email at business@tamarindhillpress.com or by phone on +44 1325 775 255
OR +44 7982 90 90 37 (WhatsApp) for more information.

TAMARiND HiLL
.PRESS
www.tamarindhillpress.com

Table of Contents

Family First

"Why does Zoya get to bring her entire school and I can't take my dog with me?" Yura complained, his hands folded across his chest, his eyes filling with tears. "It's not fair," he cried.

"Yura, the dog is not coming and that's final. We have been over this..." Yura opened his mouth to say something else but was shut down immediately, "I said, THAT...IS...FINAL."

His father walked away leaving him there at the foot of the stairs. A tear fell. Yura was tired of being treated as the least important one in his family. He never got what he wanted. In his mind, his family did not understand him and he often wished that he had been born to other parents. This was one of the times he was wishing exactly that.

He loved going camping with his family and looked forward to it, but this time, his sister was bringing friends and that would mean less attention paid to him. Ashok, his dog, never overlooked him, no matter who was around. It would have meant everything if he could have brought him along.

At the ringing of the doorbell, Yura wiped his eyes and ran up the stairs to his room. This was his way of protesting. Although, it didn't mean much. He didn't come back out until his father yelled for him to get into the car about twenty minutes later.

As they drove along the highway, noise reverberated in the vehicle; it was a wonder how anyone was hearing each other. The teenagers were extremely loud, but so were the parents in the front seats.

Twelve-year-old Yura had blocked everyone out, he was in his own world. This was his escape. Yura gazed up at the sky, while listening to some of his favourite music through his headphones. After all, there wasn't anything he could add to any of the conversations going on around him. Suddenly, his peace was interrupted by a blow to the head. It wasn't a soft one either.

"Ouch!" he squealed.

It was Jasha, Zoya's boyfriend. He liked to poke fun at Yura and often illtreated him, which he always got away with.

Zoya was an eighteen-year-old teenager, crazy in love with her first boyfriend and never defended Yura against him. His parents never ridiculed Jasha or Zoya, for fear that they would have an argument and she'd run off with Jasha. Yura had overheard his mother citing this as the reason she didn't tell her daughter Jasha was no good for her. She was pleading with her husband one day in the laundry room, begging him not to throw Jasha out of Zoya's room, though it was already dark. Yura had come down stairs to grab a snack but pretended he didn't hear the conversation. He assumed this was the same reason Jasha could do what he wanted with him. Everyone simply pretended they didn't see how much he terrorised Yura.

"Don't be a sissy. Are you bird watching?"

"Come on, leave him alone. He's just a kid," said Nadia, one of Zoya's best friends.

Yura was shocked that Nadia spoke up for him.

"I agree. Leave him alone. This little man here will grow up. If you keep treating him like this, one fine day he'll show you who's the boss," Kesar joked.

"Yeah, right. He's a sissy, he can't beat anyone up. Not even in a million years," Jasha laughed, flicking Yura's ear.

"Come on guys, we still have a long way to go. Do not start bickering," Igor interjected from the driver's seat.

"Dad, we are just messing around. No one is bickering," Zoya said, not giving her words much thought. These days, she barely did. She rubbed Jasha's leg, trying to get his attention back to her.

Yura scratched his head a little, annoyed by everyone he was surrounded by.

Why can't I just disappear and never see this family again, he thought.

He gave Jasha a dead look before putting his headphones back on. Turning back to the window, he got lost in the view of the sky above him and his music. He liked to make up stories based on the shape of the clouds; he would enjoy that for the rest of the journey if no one else bothered him.

After a couple of hours in the car, they arrived at the coveted campsite. A wide variety of trees created the backdrop of the site separating it from the highway. Colourful log cabins scattered the grounds, looking like flowers hidden between trees. You could hear the water from the falls hitting the rocks at its base from the parking area. There were people busy setting up camp here and there, some sitting outside cabins seeming quite settled in, as if they had already been there at least a day. Close to the pond, there was a group of people roasting fish over a woodfire. A dog ran up to Yura and he bent down to cuddle it. Yura could feel a bit of joy returning to his being.

Maybe this week away won't be so bad after all, he thought.

"Who's a good girl? Who's a good girl?" Yura mumbled into the Labrador's fur. "You're a good girl... Yes, you are... You're a good girl."

The Lab licked his face a nuzzled into his belly, pushing Yura to the ground. He nuzzled into him some more and Yura couldn't stop laughing.

"Tilly, no!!" a woman came running, trying to stop the dog.

"Don't worry about it," Igor said. "They are just playing. Yura couldn't take his dog along and she seems to like the company," he smiled at the red-head.

"Sorry, nonetheless," she apologised.

"Trust me, it's not a problem," Shelly added, coming around the vehicle to join her husband. "Come on, Yura; this lady needs her dog back," she said, turning to her son.

After an introduction and exchange of a bit of background information, the American from Wisconsin, Tamia, left with her dog in tow. She promised Yura that he could play with her while he was at the site, which made him very happy.

Yura snorted watching his sister. Zoya was being a giddy schoolgirl hanging on to Jasha down by the lake on the deck, instead of building her tent. He couldn't understand. He was so close with his sister before Jasha came along; now, he barely recognised her.

She loved fishing, going on excursions, playing lapta, foraging with him, and so much more. Zoya was the type of sister who would wake him up with tickles in the mornings. She was his best friend and now she barely had time to even say hello to him. If Jasha wasn't in the picture, she would be building her tent fast, trying to finish quickly so they could go fishing. Every year, she would try to beat him and the whole family at catching the biggest fish. Yura prayed he'd never stop being adventurous as Zoya had.

"Yura, keep the nail straight or you will get hurt," his father warned, bringing him out of his reverie.

"Ah, sorry."

His father hammered in one of the tent's nails, and he pinned it to the ground.

"But why do we have to work while they do what they want?" Yura whined.

"They can do what they want because they are grownups, but because they are, I will not help them to set up their tent when they want to go to sleep." The man smiled and winked at his son.

The boy was surprised, but then laughed.

"He who sleeps doesn't catch fish," Yura repeated a saying his grandpa always used.

"I couldn't agree more," Igor smiled at him.

They finished building their tent and moved everything in. Yura made it his duty to leave Zoya's tent in the vehicle so she would have to get it herself. When he went fishing with his parents, he was happy that Jasha was otherwise occupied. The only thing missing was the fun he would have had with Zoya, but he enjoyed fishing, nevertheless.

Igor caught the biggest fish, third year in a row. His wife was not so happy. She used to be the big catcher of the family but that all ended three years ago when Igor took the lead. Yura simply loved the activity and spending time with his family, he never truly cared who was better at it.

When evening was approaching and they had to settle into the tents before dinner, Zoya went to complain to her father, demanding that he help them build the tent.

The man smiled and shook his head, "If you really want a hand, then you will have to ask him," he pointed at Yura.

"What?! But he doesn't even know how to tie his shoe laces! You always build our tents. All he does is pass you the nails."

"Well, you should have been here when I was building the tents and I would have helped you with yours." The man crossed his arms.

Zoya pouted at her father's stubbornness but eventually asked her brother for help.

Yura smiled big, feeling like an important person and an adult. He looked at his father with admiration.

When Zoya returned with little Yura, the other teenagers made a joke of it.

"Why are you back with the dreamer?" Kesar laughed.

"To make us dream up a tent, right?" teased Jasha.

They laughed and made fun of him, but all Yura could think was that, without him, the four would have to sleep outside. So, he smiled, just waiting for the right moment.

"Will you put up the tent already?" asked Zoya.

Yura's face lit up with a wicked grin and he shook his head. "Well, sister dearest, I never said that I would build it, but that I would help you. Start by taking the nails and fixing them to the ground."

"Hey, watch this kid. He wants to command us like slaves," Jasha said, annoyed.

"Meanwhile, he is the only one who knows how to set up the tent," Nadia pointed out.

Jasha was a braggart and chased Yura away. They started putting up their tent, doing a poor job of it. Yura went back to his parents, annoyed with his sister's boyfriend. He just couldn't stand him.

After dinner, the teenagers sat around the fire with a guitar, singing and telling stories, all laughing and having fun.

Yura stared at them sulky and annoyed. This was his family trip. Camping was supposed to be there thing; something that the four of them could enjoy.

I've had enough of all of this, Yura complained internally. *Who do they think they are? Does Zoya think she can just discard us? We are a family; we stick together no matter what!*

"Why don't we have some fun too? Shall we all play something?" his mother asked with a smile, invading his thoughts.

"I don't feel like it."

Shelly looked at him, a little worried to see him that way. She looked at her husband as if to seek an answer, but he just shrugged.

Yura gave his sister and her friends a hostile glare. Sweat began to form on his brow as his anger grew more and more. Zoya was okay to have fun with all her friends and completely disregard him and their family traditions. As he sat there on his camp chair, not hearing a word his father and mother exchanged, he devised a plan. He would show them not to ever hijack his family camping trip ever again.

Yura got up from his chair without anyone noticing. He walked around the cabin and came up behind Zoya and her friends, the fire blazing in front of them. She was laughing with Jasha as he sang to her, throwing her arms around his neck. Like a prey, Yura came up on them, slowly and quietly. He was soon behind Kesar, no one noticing him.

Suddenly, Yura jumped out in front of the group, blocking their fire. He stood in a frightening pose, his hands coming up in front of him like a mountain bear ready to attack. He leaned forward, opening his mouth, and baring his sharp fangs. Both Zoya and her friends were frightened by his sudden appearance. Jasha pushed Zoya into him, standing from his camp chair in an instant.

"Please man, please don't hurt me," he begged, shaking in his skin.

Kesar held on to Nadia for dear life, trying to hide the fact that he had peed himself the moment Yura had appeared in front of them.

They all stared at Yura—more so at the two long canines that he did not have before—in terror.

Zoya panicked. She grabbed Yura by the arm, pulling him away from the group. Her grip was strong, her nails digging into his skin. "What are you doing?" she asked through gritted teeth. "Do you have any idea what you have just done!?" She was covered in cold sweat, afraid that her friends had seen what she had.

When Yura jumped in front of the group, his back to his parents, they both chuckled. However, as they watched the reaction of the group, and saw the terror on Zoya's face, they knew something was wrong. The two made eye contact before jumping up from their camp chairs and rushing over to their children. They looked at them confused.

Zoya immediately pulled her brother and parents to the side, agitated.

"Mom! Dad! Yura showed them!" she whispered.

"What?" Igor asked.

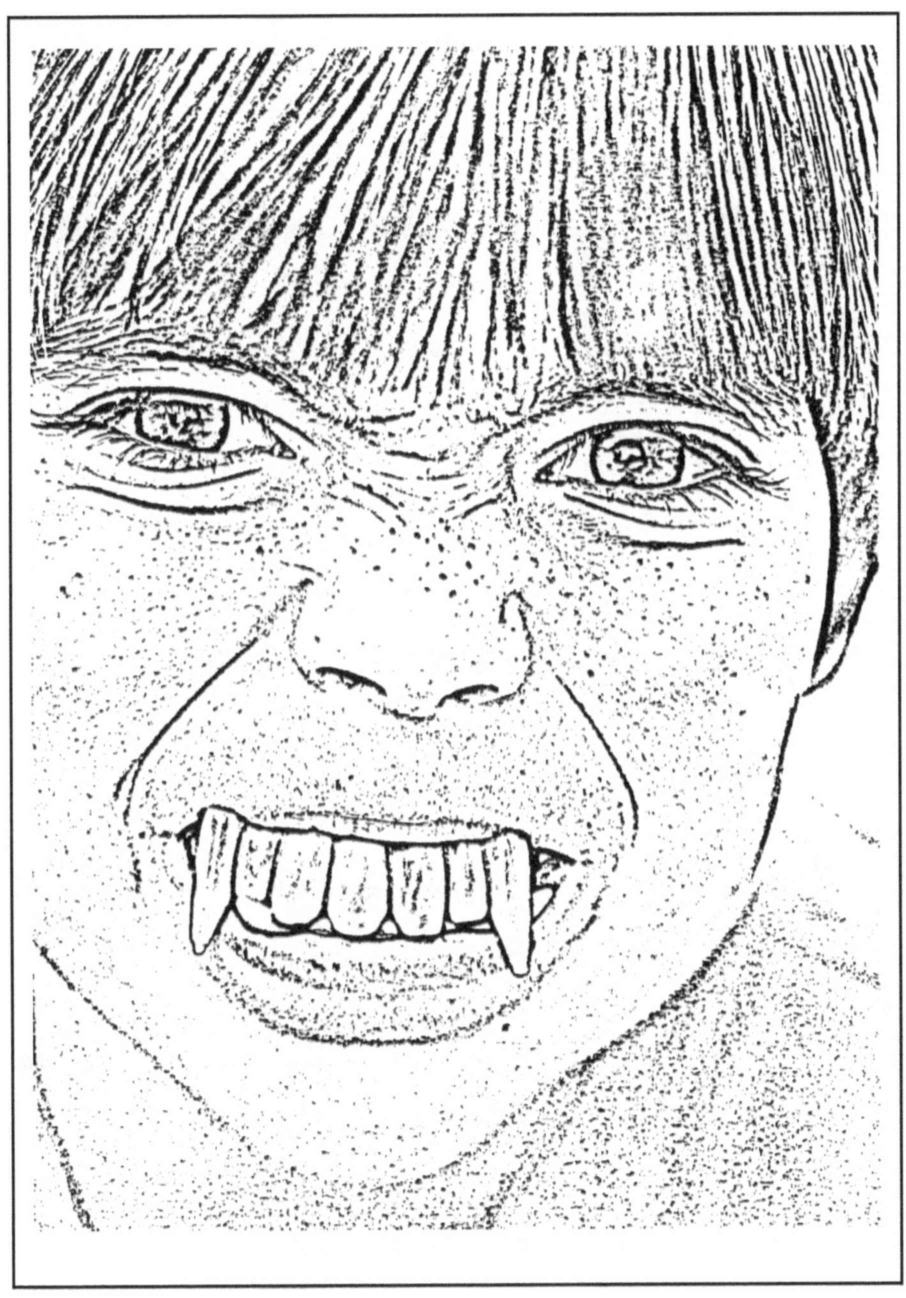

"His forsaken canines! He showed them."

The two jumped back in disbelief. They too quickly became nervous and unsettled.

"Do you think they've seen them?" Shelly asked, her voice shaky.

"I'm afraid they have," Zoya whimpered.

Zoya was petrified as were her parents. Yura on the other hand, was very pleased with himself. He didn't care that they had seen his canines. He kept replaying the picture of Jasha shaking like a leaf in his head. What a joy it was for him to see that!

"Yura! Why did you do that? And where did you get the money to buy those fake teeth? I have warned you more than once not to use your pocket money for silly things," his mother pretended to scold him. She spoke loud enough so that the three could hear them.

They started back to where the group was. Shelly faked a smile at him, even though she was hyperventilating on the inside.

"Go on, apologise," she ordered, rubbing his back.

Yura hung his head, not in shame but because he was hiding the look on his face. He was trying hard not to laugh out loud. Jasha was red, like when one gets sunburnt after being in the sun all day. Yura was relishing in the effect his actions had.

"Sorry," he muttered, trying harder not to laugh now.

"Come on, don't disturb them again, understand?" Igor scolded him, pulling Yura close to him. He was nervous. If they learned of their true nature, that would be the end of normalcy for his family. He was by no means okay with what Yura had done.

"Go to bed, now," he said in a low growl when they neared their tent.

Back at the fire, the three friends looked at the scene perplexed. "They were fake? How frightening," said Nadia, sighing.

"What the hell, that little guy gave me chills," Jasha crooned, rubbing his guitar a little.

"Kids," Kesar shook his head. There was no way he was going to stand up until everyone went to bed. He did not want anyone to know that he had peed his pants and, in all fairness, he was still terrified.

Zoya heaved a big sigh of relief. The three seemed to have bought it. "Now you all know why having a little brother is annoying," she remarked with a slight chuckle.

A couple of days went by at the campsite, and everyone was having fun and playing together. Igor, however, was still unsettled from

Yura's stunt the other night. He still kept an eye on the teens to make sure they were actually past the matter.

He noticed that Kesar, unlike Jasha and Nadia, seemed troubled. Kesar looked over his shoulder often, and at times looked very worried. Igor also noticed that whenever one of his family members were around, Kesar tried to stay to himself, as if he was trying not to attract any attention. He seemed careful even around Zoya. It was when Yura was present that Kesar appeared most frightened. This was what worried Igor the most.

Soon, the trip was over and the group headed back to their city life in the centre of Moscow. Each of Zoya's friends returned to their homes, including Jasha, finally relaxing from the trip and drive back. All but one.

Igor sat on the sofa biting his fingernail and shaking his leg. He hadn't slept in the last few days and couldn't get his mind to settle either. Something in his gut told him that Kesar didn't buy what they sold him about Yura's teeth being fake.

How could he be so stupid? Igor thought. *We can lose everything that we have worked for over the last two decades. Everything.*

Shelly called from the kitchen but there was no answer. She walked into the living room to find her husband pensive on the sofa. No wonder he couldn't hear her. He seemed quite far away.

"Honey, I've been calling you. What's going on? Is something bothering you?" asked his wife, sitting down next to him, taking his hand in hers, interrupting his nail biting.

"Shelly, I can't shake it. I'm worried about those three, especially Kesar. Something tells me he didn't believe us. That he knows that we are different... That..."

"Come on, relax. I think they all bought it. They have no idea who we are. They had so much fun at the camp. Plus, they are teenagers, they've already moved on to the next hot top—"

"But, that Kesar kid kept watching us... Like he was scared of us. Like—"

"What?" Shelly shifted on the sofa. Do you really think he knows?" There was a slight panic in her voice.

Igor didn't want her to worry. They'd spent too many years concealing their identity and did it so well. He knew that her deepest fear was having people find out and hurting her children. He thought about what his wife said. Maybe, this time she was right.

Kesar might not know anything.

If he knew that he was among them, he would not have behaved normally. In fact, he would have been petrified. There was no way he would have stayed the rest of the trip.

Igor couldn't ignore what he saw with his own eyes, though. That boy was not okay. He was not comfortable around them, especially when Yura was near.

"But, Kesar..." Igor said, suspiciously.

This time, Shelly decided to indulge her husband. "Okay, tell me exactly why you are worried," she told him.

Igor went into great detail, sharing incidents of strange behaviours from Kesar. At the time, Shelly admitted she didn't think too much of any of it. Looking back over the entire week and everything that her husband told her, she had to agree.

Kesar hadn't bought their story.

"Do you think that he understood, though? Like fully understood?"

"In my opinion, yes. When we pulled up, he didn't even take the time to say goodbye to the others."

"Oh... I noticed that. I didn't pay it any mind then but he literally went straight from our car into the cab and was gone in seconds."

"Do you think we should ask Zoya whether she's heard anything from any of them?"

"No, the kids are involved enough already. I'd prefer to just handle this on my own. It's my duty to protect my family."

Igor stopped to think about the last two decades. Well, it pretty much just flashed before his eyes. Twenty-one years ago, when he woke up in that lab to find himself with different abilities, he didn't think for once that he'd ever be able to exist in the real world again.

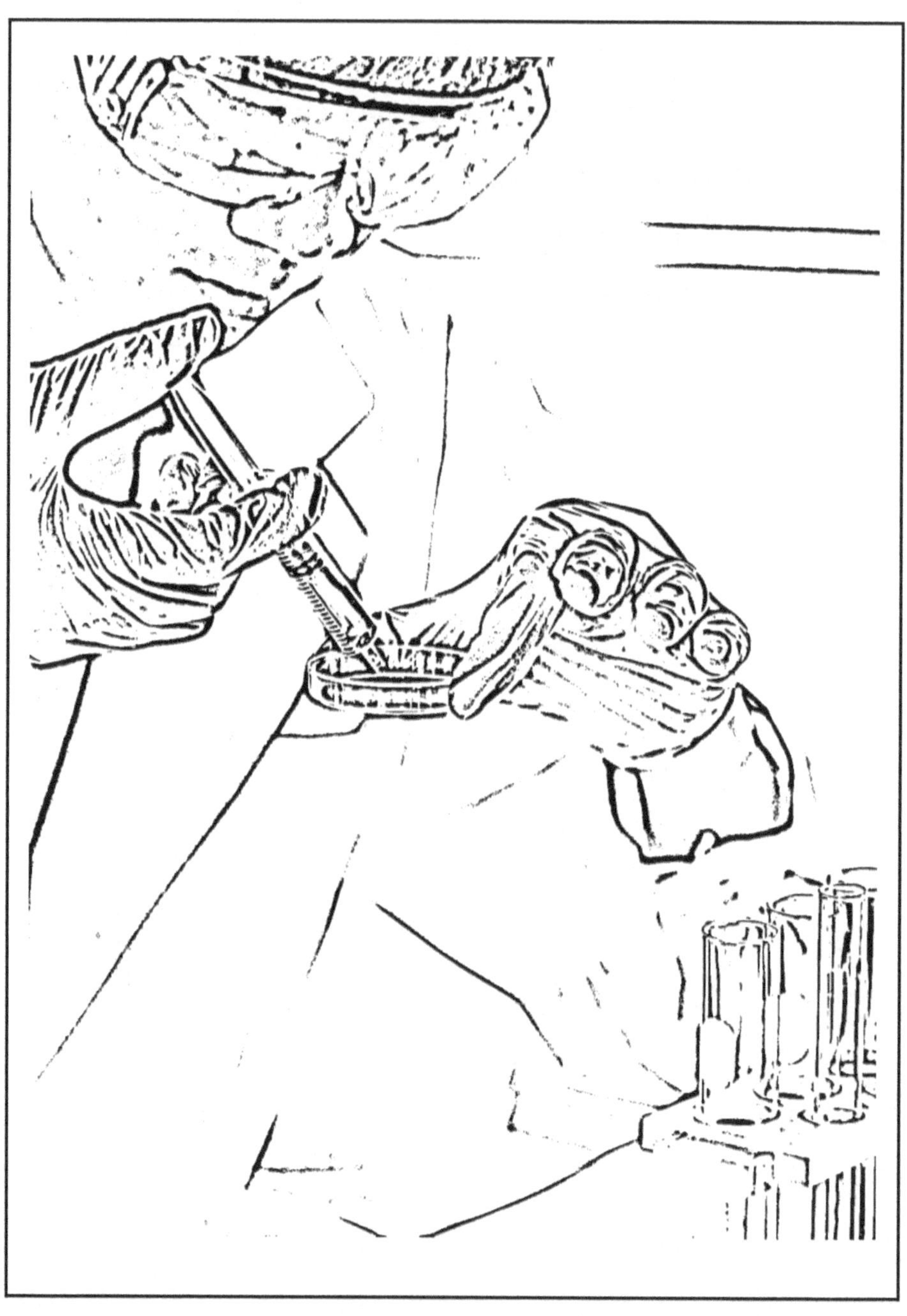

All he wanted was the money they had promised him—€700 to be exact.

He was planning to buy books for his second-year economics course. The ad said that he would be paid for the blood tests and if he could participate in the study, he would receive another pay-out of almost €20,000.00. How that would have helped with his studies.

He remembered getting to the office building and being escorted down to the basement. What happened next, he still couldn't remember to this day. All Igor knew was that he woke up in the middle of the field with a group of other people, all of whom had no idea where they were or how they had gotten there.

In the days that followed, Igor and the others realised that they were able to do things that were out of this world. One guy could jump hundreds of feet into the air and land right back on his feet with no problems whatsoever. There was a girl who could look any of them in the eyes and tell them exactly what they were thinking, word for word. Another, as did Shelly, only wanted blood. It took Igor and the others some time to get them to stop trying to eat them.

Igor seemed to have most of these abilities combined.

Like Shelly, he had characteristics of a vampire, like the canines and the crave for blood. He had the ability to make people forget things he wanted them to. However, he could control his crave for blood and, like Shelly and the other girl, could walk around in the sun all day without being burned to death. He didn't fear the smell of garlic either. In fact, to this day, he still ate foods laced with garlic, one of his favourite things to eat.

Soon, he realised he had this urge to protect Shelly and keep her safe, and the two decide to find their way back to civilization and settle together, as a couple. They made a promise to never let those around them know what they were capable of. Though it took quite some time, Shelly soon learned to control her crave for blood and had never had to suck any human dry.

They looked different physically and never made contact with their families. Shelly's family kept her missing person's case opened for years, but Shelly knew it was safe to not reconnect with them. As heart-breaking as it was for her, she knew it was best for them.

"Should I pay him a visit at least to confirm our suspicions?" Igor asked, pulling himself back to reality.

His wife paused for a moment before nodding.

"Go, we can't risk it. And if you have to, do what you must."

She lowered her head as she said the last sentence. Shelly hated hurting other people but her family was her priority. They mattered more than anything and anyone else did.

Igor nodded, then immediately left for the boy's house.

It took Igor no time to get there. He knocked on the front door, and Kesar himself came to open it. The boy shuddered in fear. He looked nervous in Igor's eyes, which he noticed right away.

"Hi Kesar, sorry to disturb you. I know that after our long journey, you probably wanted to rest. But-I-" The man smiled, as if none of his worries afflicted him.

"N-no, I'm glad to see you again. Did I leave something behind?" Kesar tried to smile, but his was a distorted one.

"No, not at all. Actually, I was just around the corner and thought I'd stop in to see if you enjoyed our trip," Igor forced a smile as he added, "because very soon we will be going on another one and I wanted to know if you would like to keep Zoya company again."

"Aah... Uhm... Jasha will be all the company she needs, don't you think?" Kesar grew more nervous. His reason for stopping by made no sense.

He knows, he flipping knows, Kesar panicked.

An idea came to mind and he spat it out in an instant. "Tha-that was my last trip for the holidays, Mr Mikheev. I got a job that I am starting this week, you know, growing up...lots of responsibilities. I need the money."

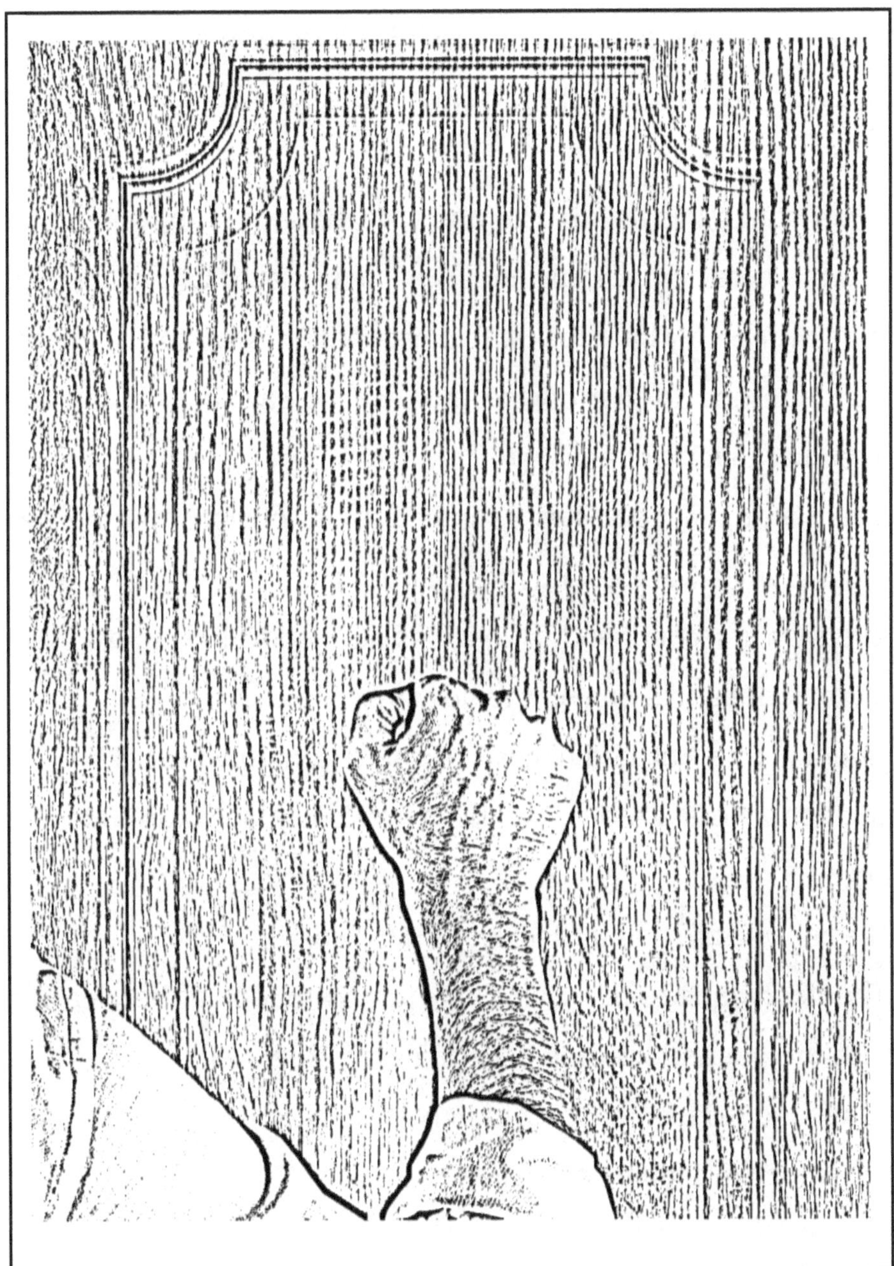

"Oh, okay, I understand. So, it isn't because of that joke my son played on you?" Igor asked, paying close attention to the boy's words.

"Your son? Which joke? The one with the ants in my shoes? Or the one where he threw my underwear in the lake? Oh, it's the one where he filled my backpack with pinecones," Kesar listed off things Yura had done to him on the trip, as if to say that he couldn't remember that night at all.

The man understood Kesar's intent, it was obvious that he was lying. His smile wavered at times, he didn't look him in the eyes for more than a second, and as much as he tried to hide it, his hand on the door handle behind the door trembled.

"Right..." Igor watched him, still suspicious, narrowing his eyes.

Suddenly, Kesar's mother, a plump and lovely lady, walked by the door.

"Kesar, who are you talking to?" she asked.

The boy jumped and instinctively turned to look at her, leaving space for Igor and his mother to see each other.

When the woman recognized him, she smiled, saying, "Aww, Mr. Mikheev, Zoya's father, right?"

The man smiled warmly. "Yes, indeed. You're Kesar's mother, right? Not that you look a day older than sixteen."

"Oh, you liar. I am aging and not like fine wine," she chuckled. "Glad you are here. I wanted to thank you for taking my son camping with your family. You know, without a man in the house and all my health issues, I can't do much to keep up with a teenage boy."

Kesar became anxious and tried to call his mother back. "Mom, I already thanked him. He knows..."

The woman didn't listen to him and continued to approach Igor.

"You know, he's pretty much part of our family. He's been friends with Zoya since when; K1?"

"Yes, yes," she laughed. "They pretty much grew up together, isn't it?"

"I take the kids camping every year. Even if it takes all day to get there and set up, spending time in nature is really invigorating. We enjoy it as a family." All this while, Igor kept his foot carefully outside the door.

"Exactly. Poor Kesar doesn't have many opportunities to interact with mother nature. That's why I was so happy that you took him with."

"Thank goodness then. I'm glad this experience has helped him." Igor smiled at Kesar.

"Mom, please..." the boy was almost in tears. He wanted in every way to try to get his mother away from that man.

"By the way, Mr. Mikheev, since you and your family have been so kind to take care of my boy, can I offer you some of my special beef stroganoff to thank you?"

"Of course, I would gladly accept it, ma'am." This was it. Igor was about to get just what he wanted.

"How nice! Come in, come in. Make yourself comfortable while I prepare it." The woman happily skipped to the kitchen, grateful for adult company. Kesar wasn't the only one who could do with some attention.

Kesar trembled with fear from his mother's words. As if water had been poured right over his head, heavy beads of sweat appeared on his forehead. He looked at Igor with terror in his eyes.

Igor smiled, lowering his head disturbingly, a shadow suddenly covering his face. "Thank you very much." His voice seemed lower than usual as his foot came over the threshold.

Kesar visibly shivered in fright, his eyes wet with tears. He almost wet his underwear. The sight of Yura jumping in front of them by the campfire was front and centre in his mind.

When Igor took the first step into the house and saw that nothing happened to him, he followed with the other foot. Since he had received permission from the owner, and the house was considered a sacred place for everyone, entering Kesar's home did not cause him any trouble at all. Igor smiled at that; now they were easy prey. Now it was time to protect his family, just as he had promised his wife over eighteen years ago when Zoya was born; at all costs.

Kesar's knees began to buckle. The fear was stronger than him, he backed away, falling. He pulled himself up quickly and raced upstairs, disappearing from Igor's view. He slammed the door of his room and locked it.

Igor followed him with his eyes until he disappeared behind the column of the banister. He didn't see where he went exactly but knew that the boy wasn't safe from him, not after he was invited into the house. Kesar's mother didn't react to the banging of the door upstairs, she was used to it. Igor locked the front door, putting the keys into his pocket.

"Come in, dear, I doubled the portion for your family! I hope they all enjoy it," Kesar's mother said from the kitchen.

"I'll be right there," Igor said menacingly, his canines struggling to remain tucked away. His voice became hoarser and lower, "I'll be right there," he growled.

His canines were now out and his breathing became like that of a wild animal on the hunt.

There was a deep guttural growl. A bellowing scream echoed through the air. The birds in the garden took flight in an instant.

Then everything went quiet.

Moments later, Igor exited the house. He spotted a speck of blood on his wrist and quickly wiped it away. He looked up and down the street before getting into his car and driving away.

His family was safe again.

Hopefully...

Don't Go Live

"The big social media influencer, Ashley-kins..."

"Internet star, Ashley-kins..."

The father of a small family was quickly flipping through channels on their smart TV. They were shocked to see that all the shows were talking about the same thing.

David turned off the TV and turned to his daughter, "What the hell got into you?! How could you jeopardise our lives like this? All for fame!"

The girl was pale and really didn't know what to do. "I-I... I'm sorry!"

"Your empty apologies will get you nowhere! Do you realize the trouble you've got us into?!"

"Come on, dear, calm down. Getting angry is useless," the mother, Amy, interjected. Then she looked at her daughter and said, "Ashley, know that we're very upset about what you have done, but for now, we have to safeguard ourselves. You will be dealt with later. Now, take your grandmother and go down to the bunker. Your father and I will take the bare essentials down in a few."

They were all angry, and frightened, but David nodded at his wife in agreement. Now was not the time to fight. They had to stick together.

🐺

<u>One day earlier</u>

In New York, New York, a young CrewViewer who went by the name Ashley-kins had just gone live on her channel with millions of viewers tuning in. She'd been online for only a few minutes when she'd hit 3.2 million viewers. This wasn't a huge audience for her. Within the first ten minutes of each of her lives, she'd normally hit over 12 million on a good day.

"...for your package. And let me just remind everyone that you can send me packages. All the deets are in the description below this video, or any of the others of course," she chuckled, winking into the camera. "Come on guys, don't keep me all to yourself now. Invite all your friends to the live so we can all hang out. While you do that, let me open another friend's package..."

She reached down and took one up from the floor. "Awww, LuckyU, thanks for your gift... Oooh, what could it be?" Ashley wondered, ripping the package open with her carefully manicured nails. She had on coffin shaped tips painted in blue and gold. Her middle fingernails each had a sculpted bear on them. This was one of the things her followers liked about her. Her nails were always well done and looked cute.

"Friends, you will not believe what I have here! It's a taser," she said, pulling it out of the box. She saw what it was pretty much the same time her audience did. The confused girl chuckled, "To defend myself against the attackers I guess," she shrugged. "Thank you very much, I'll treasure it. But how does it work?"

She curiously moved the taser. Instantaneously, it discharged and a strong voltage charged through her. Ashley lost control of her body for a full second, but at that moment, her face took on a weird shape. Her left hand, the hidden one, slightly took the shape of a clawed hand.

Ashley threw the taser on the ground, trembling and in shock. It was only then that she realised that she had shifted for a second. In a panic, she ended the live immediately, without saying another word.

She breathed heavily, not only from the shock of before, but also because of anxiety. She was having a panic attack. *What have I done?* Her breathing grew more laboured. She was sweating, especially her palms. Ashley bent over trying to compose herself. She rested her forehead on her knees and hugged herself the way she'd practised many times before. "They...must...have...all...seen...me..." she wheezed.

Ashley needed to fix this; her whole world would turn upside down otherwise. How was she ever going to undo this? She was live and millions of people had seen her. *That's it,* she thought. *Yes, it will be like it never happened.*

She struggled to move but was soon able to get herself in an upright position again. Ashley busied herself with her laptop. The video was still there on her channel. An air of relief washed over her as she hit the confirm button. The video was gone. Ashley said a quick prayer in her mind. *There, fixed. I fixed it.*

"Okay," she said aloud, "no need to panic. Problem averted. I deleted it. Soon everyone will forget about it and everything will be fine again."

Would it be though? What would the world do now that they had seen her? The internet was unpredictable. From the moment she stepped into the world of social media, Ashley had been loved by fans all over the world. Girls wanted to be her or date her and it was the exact same with boys. She was one of the few CrewViewers who never felt the wrath of trolls and keyboard bullies. One thing she knew for sure was that once they started, there was no way of getting *untrolled.* It would last forever and, like most, she would have to shut down her channel and leave social media all together in order to escape them. Ashely hoped with all her might that this would just go away.

I need to leave this room; otherwise, I will lose my mind, Ashley told herself.

Taking a few deep breaths, she tried to calm herself down some more. She walked up to her bedroom door and wrapped her fingers around the handle. Before she turned it, she took another deep breath and checked herself in the mirror on the wall next to her. She didn't want her family to know something was wrong. Forcing a smile at herself in the mirror, she said, "This never happened. I deleted the video and tomorrow everything will go back to normal." Ashley turned the handle and left her room.

The next few hours took her mind off what had happened. She spent the rest of the evening with her family, even helping her mother prepare dinner.

Present Day - Morning

Ashley had woken up with a start. She could hear voices in the house, almost like an argument. She covered her head with her pillow, wondering what her parents were fussing about this time. She rolled over and reached for her phone. In an instant, her eyes went owl-wide. Ashley shot up in her bed, pushing her hair out of her face, staring at the phone in her hand.

"No, no, no, no;" she became unnerved.

She couldn't even read the number clearly! There were too many. She had notifications on all her socials. Ashley's hand was shaking. She struggled to get her phone to read her fingerprint. What she saw when she got onto one platform stunned her. The video was shared over 100 million times! What was going on, she had deleted it. She was sure. Ashley almost fell off the bed rushing to her computer. She went onto CrewView and made sure it was no longer there and it wasn't. She went on social media to see exactly what was being passed around. It was a video only twenty-three seconds long but it was there. Right there in the video she saw what everyone was freaking out about. She shifted. That part only lasted about two seconds but there was no denying it.

Ashely started crying and pulling on her hair slightly. What had she done? How as she going to fix this? People needed an explanation and they weren't being quiet about it. So many speculations were being passed around.

'She's playing a prank on all of us!' one comment read.

'I wonder how she did the graphics for that?' another commented asked.

'I knew we weren't alone on earth!!! How long have I been saying this?!! This is proof!'

'She is a freak!! She shouldn't be allowed to mix with us. Where does she live!!!'

There were mixed emotions but a lot of people were angry.

Ashley paled at the situation. She shivered with fear. She knew that this could endanger her family and surely her parents would be mad to death with her. If their secret was revealed, it would mean no more living among humans: no social media, the comfort of a house, eating out at restaurants, nor the company of her friends. Everything would be lost—everything! Not only that, could they get out on time?

Ashley sat at her desk blocking as many people as she could, for almost an hour. She still couldn't tell what her parents were arguing about but they were still arguing since she had woken up. She tried to hide away in her room but was soon summoned downstairs by her father.

"Ashley! Get down here now!"

About Ten Minutes Earlier

Ashley let out a big sigh and clutched her chest. She was beyond panicking now. The tone of her father's voice drove so much fear into her.

"Now! Get down here now!" David screamed when he didn't hear her door open immediately.

"Ashley," her mother called.

"Co-coming," Ashley replied, her voice trembling.

"Now!" her father boomed; Ashley was sure that the whole house trembled in that instant.

Ashley was physically shaking, she felt she was about to puke her guts out. Her legs felt as though they were going to buckle. She wished the floor would open up and swallow her whole. The stress was causing her to shift in and out of form and it was making things worse. She felt lightheaded. Ashley held onto the foot of her gold framed metal bed to gather her strength. Putting one foot in front of the other, slowly, and intentionally, she tried to get to her door.

"Ashley-kins, a werewolf among us?" she heard a news lady saying as her foot hit the very last step. Her parents turned and looked at her as she appeared in the doorway of their living room.

Her father stepped forward in rage but quickly collected himself, standing in place. Ashley flinched at that, cowering at that. Her mother was in tears.

"Look what you have done!" David cried as he turned to the TV above the fireplace, flipping from channel to channel.

Despite her best efforts, the video was still circulating, and she couldn't do anything to stop it. Within a few hours, it had gained so much popularity and was still trending on all social media networks. Everyone was talking about it. The speculations were relentless and tension was building.

Suddenly, there was a knock at her front door. It was followed by another, then another. They all ignored it—Ashley visibly frightened.

"Your father and I will take the bare essentials down in a few," her mother finished.

Ashley pushed herself to follow her parents' instructions.

Present Time

Amy and David packed up a few things including their two rifles and went to the bunker/basement to join the others. Amy was trying to hide her true feelings. She was angry with her daughter, very much so. However, the wellbeing of her family was what was important now.

"Mom, can you just move over a bit, I need to get something off the shelf behind you," Amy said.

Grandma-Rachel moved out of her daughter's way.

David was pacing the room. "One rule, I had one simple rule, and you couldn't follow it. Just one rule: Do not get discovered. Ever!"

Ashley was crying, feeling guilty about everything. She was hyperventilating, frightened, and anxious.

"Don't yell at her," Grandma-Rachel interjected. "You know very well that this wasn't her fault, it was that toy."

"What the hell, Mom! Do you realize the situation we're in?!" David screamed. You could see that he, too, didn't know what to do.

"Can we all just calm down! Now is not the time for us to be going against each other. We are all in this, all of us. You, David, sit down and stop with all the antics. You are not making the situation any better."

Amy placed a tablet in the middle of all of them with a broadcast on. "Let's see what's happening now."

"...uld seem that the latest speculations are right about social media influencer, who goes by the name Ashley-kins. The video has been analysed and has been proven not to be graphics of any kind. What the experts are saying is that she is indeed a werewolf. Today, we will be talking to Dr. Andrew Smith from the University of Delta Beta who is leading the research team on this. Dr. Smith, can you talk to us more about what your team has discovered and how you were able to come to your most recent conclusion?"

The doctor went on to talk about their findings, disclosing the fact that they had always known that werewolves were real. He explained that this was the first time they had found someone who managed to conceal themselves so well in society, living as humans do.

LIVE
BREAKING
NEWS

As the news continued, Grandma-Rachel became visibly worried. She was more concerned for her nineteen-year-old granddaughter who had not lived enough life yet. She liked the fact that Ashley had started her channel and was doing well. Grandma-Rachel saw how much joy it brought her granddaughter and couldn't wish for anything more. Now, all she could think about was the fact that not only was that going to be taken from her, but any and all traces of normalcy were also under threat. They couldn't just move to a new neighbourhood; her face was everywhere and everyone would know her. Their only option was to remain in the two roomed bunker they had built or find a way to escape to the forest somewhere. She worried about the idea of both for Ashley who was so used to the comforts that a human existence brought with it.

"It's everywhere. They know. They'll do away with us. What are we going to do?"

"Come on, Amy... That man is just a fanatic. They are just guessing. They can't be claiming they have proven anything. Did any of them come to this house to test you? I know for sure I didn't get tested by anyone. So, calm down. Let's all put our heads together to see how we will get through this."

"There's no getting through this, can't you see?! Our lives are ruined! I wish you hadn't encouraged her to keep making those damn videos! Look what she's done!"

"If you had paid her an ounce of attention, she wouldn't have started making those videos to begin with. So don't start throwing out blame and don't you dare take that tone with me again."

Like a small child, David cowered. Amy stepped over to his side of the coffee table and rubbed his back. She knew exactly what he felt in that moment. They were Ashley's parents, adults, but Rachel being Amy's mother and David's mother-in-law, they often felt like children whenever they stepped out of line.

"David, lead this family. Take control of yourself and this family. Now, come along; let's figure out what our next move will be," Grandma-Rachel said in a less stern voice.

"I-I- O-"

David was interrupted by what the doctor was saying on the news. His ears perked up, as did everyone else's.

"... the result of hours of research. We combed through her channel because we needed more than what was in that very short video that has been going around. It took a team of twelve and several hours of just watching CrewView videos that we have no interest in, but we stumbled upon what we really needed."

"I'm being told that we have that video here," the news agent interjected. "Can we show that video now?"

The video took over the entire TV screen. In it was the video of a Halloween party. There were a group of young people obviously having a good time. Lights were flashing and the shadows of people kept coming in and out of view. Then the camera turned to what looked like a werewolf. Ashely quickly realised what was happening and so did her parents. Her grandmother gasped and her hand flew up covering her mouth. The video ended with the werewolf on the screen.

"Dr. Smith, what are we looking at other than a bunch of teenagers having a good time at a party?"

"How could you?" Amy breathed out.

"I'm so—"

"Stop!" David shouted. "Just stop." The tone of his voice came to a murmur. Tears fell from his eyes as he rested his chin on his locked hands.

"Ashley, I am disappointed in you. You jeopardized all our lives by going to that party in your werewolf form. All our lives. There's no way we will survive this." Ashley could hear the disappointment in her mother's voice and that was like a kick in the gut.

"I just thought that it would be okay for Halloween. No one knew it wasn't a costume."

On hearing this, Amy turned bright red, steaming with rage.

"Ashley!" exclaimed her father in exasperation. "Stop talking! You have killed all of us. Your entire family. Stop making excuses. I do not want to hear one more word out of you." He didn't care what his mother-in-law would say. He'd had enough. He seemed almost ready to burst. He clenched his fists so tightly that blood dripped from his hands, his paws threatening to make themselves visible.

Ashley trembled at the sight of how angry her father was. She hid behind her grandmother, afraid of the man.

"That's enough!" her grandmother said, raising her voice slightly. "We're a family, and even if Ashley was the one who got us all into this trouble, you cannot keep getting upset with her. We have to stick together in this," she scolded him through gritted teeth.

"Daddy, I can make this right... I... I could make a video explaining that it was all a joke, or a prank," said a fearful Ashley, rubbing her hands together.

"No! No more videos! You won't endanger our family any more than you have already done!"

"But it could work," her mother interjected, "she could just explain that it's all just a big misunderstanding."

"It won't work, Amy! It will only make matters worse!"

"Well, we don't have many other options right now. Either we lead the wave by diving in too, or we let it swallow us."

Everyone went silent for a few seconds, each thinking about whether Ashley's plan could work. Finally, David sighed and looked at his daughter hopeful, but also tired. "Okay, do it," he finally said. Everyone's head turned to him almost at the exact same time, looking at him in complete shock. Grandma-Rachel was the most astonished by this.

"Are you sure you want her to do this? If this backfires, it is on all of us. You cannot keep blaming just her. But I think it's our best bet." It was her grandmother who spoke.

"We don't have any other option at this time, Mom," David responded.

"So, we are all in this together? Whatever happens from here is on all of us?" David nodded a yes at his mother-in-law in response.

Ashley was moved by the trust placed in her, and the fact that her father was finally on the same page with the rest of her family, wanting to help her fix it. She was determined to resolve the situation, one way or another.

Ashley's father climbed the steep stairs from the bunker, pushing the steel door open and climbing out. It was pitch black. David counted the twelve steps it took to get to where he wanted to be. He pushed a button on the back of the tall mop cupboard and it rotated with him standing on the base, bringing him into the kitchen. David saw a shadow pass the living room window ahead of him and ducked down. He waited a minute or so before he started moving again. Crawling on the floor, he made his way through the dining room towards the back of the house, then started up the stairs to Ashley's bedroom.

After a few minutes, he was back in the bunker with his family. David's heart was racing, he was happy he was safe downstairs again. He decided not to tell his family that someone was in their front yard.

"Thanks, Daddy," Ashley said, taking her laptop.

She pulled out the middle stool and sat by the counter facing the small kitchenette. Logging into her computer, she linked her phone and started a live video.

Like bees to honey, viewers started pouring in. In less than a minute, Ashley had hit over ten million views. This had never happened before. She knew it was because she went viral. Her heart was pounding, *Can I really pull this off? I can't do this, I can't!* she panicked internally.

Message after message kept coming at her but she paid them no attention. She didn't want to know what people were saying about her. The messages were mixed, with her fans saying it's a prank, some saying it's a conspiracy to get her to lose her following. Most of her new viewers, however, were out for blood. *Eye on the ball,* she told herself.

Ashley removed the fur from her phone camera after smacking her lips and fluffing her hair, trying to look as unbothered as she possibly could.

"Followers, new viewers, guys and gals, universe, welcome to another live with yours truly," she smiled big and pointed both thumbs at herself, "Ashleeeeeeeey-kins." She did her usual pout at the end, followed by a kiss. She was surprised at how she'd just gotten into character amidst everything that was going on. Ashley shifted on the stool, and continued talking, "Am I the only one who has seen the viral video and everything else going around on social media regarding little, old me?" she chuckled. "Like, really—a werewolf? Why didn't they say vampire? That would have been much cooler. Don't you guys think? The things people do to tear others down."

Ashley didn't want to show any fear or deceit; she needed to fix things. There was no way she would allow her stupidity to ruin her family's existence. She kept a straight face and kept going.

"I know there are a lot of rumours going around about me right now, but before the situation gets out of control, I have decided to explain. What you saw was not a transformation or shift or whatever they are calling it. It was nothing more than a filter which I was trying out. I thought it would be cool, you know. But now I realise what a chaos it has caused, all I can do is apologise." She tried to look as apologetic as she could.

"And I know you all may be thinking, 'But it was live, how can this be editing?' It's not editing as such. It's like one of those QuickChat filters. Got it from a new tech guy I'm trying to work with. I didn't actually intend to use it then but when that silly thing almost fried me, I touched the button and ended up turning it on for a brief moment."

Suddenly, Ashley thought to give them what she knew they would need—proof.

"Look, I'll show you." She did really have a new filtering app that she was going to be promoting soon. She was waiting on the contracts to be finalised and for the first payment to hit her bank account. She was using it to film that very video but none of the filters were turned on. She used the app to switch from filter to filter—first an angel, then she was a unicorn, then a smiling dog—she kept changing the filter. Eventually, she initiated her shift and for a brief moment, a werewolf appeared on the screen in front of everyone.

"See, just a filter." She turned on the filter with the halo and stuck to that one as she continued her video. "Let me just say sorry if this bothered any of you. It was just supposed to be fun and I wanted to use it for a video in the future after explaining to you guys. Mistakes happen and this was just one of them. I apologize again. And to all the doctors and news reporters out there trying to spin a story and make a big buck, make me a vampire... That's far cooler. To my loyal followers, don't let this get to you. We are millions strong and still counting, see you soon," she kissed the camera. "I'm out!"

The whole family was gathered around the tablet to see how the world was reacting to the video as she was filming. Her mother was focussed on the comments. David was too busy hyperventilating still.

'You liar!'

'I used something similar for Halloween. She's telling the truth!'

'All of this over a stupid filter?'

'But that doctor said he did research. Who knows who to believe these days?'

'This is just a publicity stunt to get her more followers! Booooo!'

'Who are you kidding?'

'LoL @ vampire! You rock Ashley!!!'

'Let the doctors test you so we can get the proof we need. No one believes this crap.'

It was that last comment that made Amy's face turn tomato red. Her eyes wide, her hands trembling in an instant.

"Hon, what is it? What are you looking at?"

David looked at the screen. He didn't see the comment because so many had come after but the couple he saw were just as bad. "We're in the shit..." he complained. "There's no getting out of this, none whatsoever."

"Don't say that. We'll find a solution," his mother-in-law tried to reassure him.

"But what solution...?" the man cried. That brought Amy back to reality. "We're all doomed..." he put his hands on his face in desperation.

Ashley was surprised at his behaviour. Hadn't she just fixed everything? She hadn't read any of the comments.

Her loyal followers who were still with her seemed to mostly believe it was all a hoax. However, for more than 80% of the people on her live, what the doctor said was more plausible.

It dawned on her that her family was watching the live the entire time. They must have been panicking because of the responses to the live. A panic attack was coming on again. It was all her fault, and despite her trying to fix it, maybe she had only made things worse.

"Ashley, come over here, sweetheart. Help me find some blueberries for your father," her grandmother called.

Ashley got up, willing her body to move.

"There aren't any down here. I didn't take too much from the fridge. No fruits at all. I don't think they come in a can either," replied Amy, rubbing her husband's back.

"We need to give him something sweet. That always helps when he gets like this."

"Mom, he's never been like this."

"How do you think he got through your labour, or that time when he thought we were going to lose the house, or...?"

Amy looked at her surprised. How did she not know this about her husband?

"Exactly. There must still be some in the kitchen. I'm going to look."

"Mom, I don't want them. They won't help with this and it's not safe to go out there."

"You need them and no one knows where we live let alone to come to the house. I'm not even sure why we came down here in the first place. You sit there and try to calm down. I'll just grab them from the fridge and be back in a flash."

Ashley was completely out of it. Everything was happening around her without her being aware. She was not in touch with reality.

Stubborn as she was, Grandma-Rachel went up the stairs, leaving the others. She found herself in the darkened space and just like her son-in-law had done earlier, she counted twelve steps before stretching her hand out to find the button. She followed all the same steps and was soon in the kitchen.

While they waited, the disheartened family did not exchange a single word. Her parents on the couch, Ashley still frozen in place. Suddenly, Ashley's hearth thumped in her chest and they all heard a loud noise, as if a window had broken. A thud followed.

They were immediately alarmed. The noises came from within the house—Grandma-Rachel was in there!

Ashley was the first to move. She raced up the stairs two at a time, her parents following swiftly behind her. Ashley froze when her eyes fell upon the scene causing her father to almost trip over her. When Amy got into the room, she ran over to her mother's side, falling in a heap beside her.

"No!!!" Amy bellowed, her voice fading to a guttural tone. She raised her mother up, blood colouring her hands. Amy pulled her mother close, cradling her head to her bosom and she let out another blood curdling scream. "I will kill all of them," she said, almost inaudible.

David inspected the scene around them. His mother-in-law was bleeding from a head wound. It was evident that it had been caused by the brick lying close to her. Shards of glass littered the floor.

Ashley was now kneeling next to her mother; it was only then that she was able to hear her grandmother's groans. "Mom, let go. I need to help her," Ashley said.

Amy was staring blankly at her daughter.

"Mom, give her to me," Ashley tried to get her attention again.

She still didn't let go. Ashley put the dishtowel on the floor next to her.

"Mom," she coaxed her again. "Grandma needs help, let me help her." She held her grandmother's head in her right hand and used her left to remove her mother's arms from around her. Amy was crying now, tears dripping down from her to her mother. "That's it," Ashley said, "let her go."

"I'm going to kill them all," Amy said before letting go completely.

Ashley rested her grandmother's head on her lap, placing pressure on the wound on her head with the dishtowel. Her grandmother was wheezing in pain. "You're gonna be okay, Grandma. See, I'll make it better." A tear fell from her eye onto her grandmother's cheek. Ashley fought back the tears.

Her mother was now standing by the bay window next to her father looking out into the street. The street was littered with people and news vans. Neighbours standing on their steps staring, Mr Daniel sat on his, aiming a rifle at their house.

David was growling. Ashley looked towards her parents as another brick came flying through the window. It was only then that she heard the commotion outside. David's eyes followed the brick that had only missed his wife by a few inches. He clenched his teeth as his paws made their way to the surface. Another brick came through the window, then another, followed by another—

At lightning speed, David's clothes shredded and he transformed into a gigantic wolf. He pressed his paws up to the windowsill and his wife opened the front door before ripping her dress open with both hands and transforming herself. Compared to her husband's black-peppered coat, hers was and mixture of black and brown on her back and legs, her belly more grey. Her paws a greyish white. Ashley watched her parents knowing she needed to join them but she didn't want to leave her grandmother. She didn't want her to die because of what she had done.

Loud shouts could be heard from the street and bricks came through the door one after the other. Her mother eyed her father in her wolf form, signalling that her plan had worked.

He nudged her with his nose and stared into her eyes before they both took up positions on opposite sides of the window. They looked at each other again, then both of them went through the window: Amy landing on top of a news van, David knocking down a man with a brick at the ready. He went after Mr Daniels and in one swift movement, ripped the gun from his hand. The neighbour clutched his bleeding hand, holding it to his chest, retreating into his house backwards.

Screams of fear and terror flooded the streets as people ran into all directions in search of safety. Amy rapped on the roof of the news van, digging her paws into the roof. It worked, everyone dispersed from outside her house. David tore into one threat after another. When he went to attack a man holding what looked like a sword, his daughter cried out:

"Dad! Stop, this is what they want. To make us monsters. We are not monsters, you taught me that..."

The man with the sword in hand and two others with pickaxes advanced in David's direction.

Ashley was covering her eyes with both hands. She did not notice—she was wishing she had never made one video to begin with.

Her grandmother whimpered behind her and she opened her eyes to see that they were about to kill her father. "Daddy, she screamed. Watch out!"

David got rid of all three of them in an instant.

Ashley was back at her grandmother's side. "Please hang on, Grandma-Rachel. We are going to get you some help. Hold on, please." She was crying.

Her grandmother gave her a weak smile and with all the strength she had left, she reached up and brushed Ashley's cheek. Her eyes spoke, though she couldn't. Ashley sobbed but dug deep and gathered the strength she needed.

Ashley stood and went over to the L-shaped sofa and grabbed the red blanket thrown over the back of it. She marched back over to her grandmother, placing the blanket open on the floor next to her. She bent at the knees, reaching down and cradling her grandmother in her arms. Ashley laid her grandmother down and wrapped her in the blanket. She made her way towards the front door: the sound of shrieks penetrating her ears. She did not want to see what was happening outside.

As she made her way to the front door, carrying her grandmother, she started humming. Soon, words escaped her lips and the closer she got to the door, the louder she became.

It was her father who stopped first. He was mid-air, going after two men who were trying to attack him. He landed on all fours and looked towards his house to see his daughter coming down the front steps. Her mother growled at the group advancing towards her, stopping them in their tracks. As Amy heard the song, she too turned to look at her daughter.

It was the song they sang to her before bedtime for years, when she was still their little baby girl. Their innocent girl full of so many possibilities. As Amy looked at the vision of her daughter, and what she was sure was her mother wrapped in the blanket, she knew the life she once knew was no more.

Ashley turned left of the house, everyone frozen in their tracks. Her parents joined each other on the pavement and both followed after her.

They disappeared down the street out of everyone's view.

The family was never to be seen again.

Many said they had been killed. Others speculated that they had been captured by the government...

The truth is that the family managed to escape the city, settling with their own kind up in the mountains of Salt Lake City.

The Pack

The bell rang to mark the end of the morning's lessons. Students quickly filed through the corridors to go on their lunch break.

As they always did, the teachers stood in the doorways of their classrooms waiting for the halls to clear. They only went to lunch when all the students had dispersed from the classrooms and hallways. They checked on the students as they passed by. The order of things was the same today.

The usual group of friends who attracted their attention the most was the last to clear the hallways.

Five students, always together.

Mrs McKinley walked over to Miss Lynn as soon as the group passed them. "Look at those five. They're so sweet when they're all together like that. They remind me a lot of my youth," she mused.

"They seem to almost live in symbiosis. I've never seen any of them alone," the math teacher replied as she sipped her water.

"Teens, you know how they all form their little groups in school. I was like that at their age. But surely not half as popular," Mrs

McKinley added, reminiscing on her youth. She was about to add more...

A few of the other teachers were walking in their direction when a loud *BANG* was heard in the cafeteria. Almost instantly, they turned on their heels and ran towards the noise, all the other teachers following their lead. It was Mr Stobbart who got to the cafeteria first.

Mary-Ann was flat on her back on the ground, her tray of food scattered around her. There were oohs and ahhs in the room but none of the other students, not even her friends, were helping her up.

Mr Stobbart and another two teachers ran towards her.

"Are you okay?" Mr Stobbart asked.

"OMG! Because of this weirdo, I fell and ruined my beautiful dress!" she screamed, turning her head to stare daggers at a boy who was stood trembling in fear. The tray in his hands was cackling from the items on it shaking.

Elizabeth walked towards the boy, "You stupid fool! How—"

One of the boy's friends cut her off, "Accidents do happen you know."

"Shut it, you dimwit!" she screamed her response. The rest of her friends joined in and a shouting match ensued. Well, more like Mary-Ann's friends shouting at the group.

Charlie had disappeared by then. There was no way he was going to wait around for everyone to turn their attention back to him.

Mary-Ann was on her feet again; she'd been helped up by the two female teachers. "Him and his stupid backpack! Is he bringing his whole entire house to school with him? What does he need such a big bag for?" she yelled at no one in particular. She was furious.

Mr Stobbart rolled his eyes internally. He couldn't stand Mary-Ann and the rest of her group. In his mind, they were just a bunch of overprivileged kids who thought the world should wait on them hands and feet. No different from the kids he'd go to school with. He hated that they lacked any form of humility. He was thinking of how annoying their parents must be when, suddenly, he heard what he was waiting for all along.

"Enough, all of you!" Mr Daniels yelled, and silence fell upon the room instantly. "Every single one of you, detention this afternoon."

Murmurs began to fill the air but he raised a hand and everyone went quiet again.

"Where is Charlie?"

Teachers and students alike scanned the room for him but he was nowhere to be found. His friends exchanged glances, knowing exactly where he was.

Nevertheless, detention was set and the whole cafeteria full of students wondered whether they were in for it too but they were all too afraid to ask. If there was one thing, they all respected Mr Daniels and didn't want to be seen as defiant by him, so they dear not tried to object. They would show up and rather be told that they weren't included after school.

"Weirdos!" Mary-Ann yelled as the group of four left the cafeteria together to go find Charlie.

Emily gave her a dead stare as she left with her friends. She wanted Mary-Ann to know that she wasn't afraid of her.

When the last bell rang signalling the end of classes for the day, the assigned teachers went to the detention room. They allowed the students to come in and settle down—sending home more than ninety-nine percent of the school—before Miss Bernard was left alone with them.

Mr Daniels had called a short meeting outside the cafeteria, letting the teachers know that he feared the entire school would turn up for detention. He asked them not to clarify as he hoped the fear of seeing him again after school would keep everyone on their best behaviour for the rest of the day. He wasn't in the mood for putting out any more fires for the day.

Everything was going well in detention, until Miss Bernard decided to go to her classroom to collect some test papers that she wanted to mark in the meantime.

When she returned, she stopped dead in her tracks, stunned to find a small group gathered at the door of the room. They just stood staring her down.

She was confused by the situation, almost incredulous. She even turned to look for someone to point out the same thing to her, but it was only her there.

She went closer, still a little confused, but she smiled as she spoke. "Hey, guys... Uhm... What are you all doing out here? Waiting for your friend?" They all looked at her and nodded at the same time—emotionless.

Miss Bernard went pale, and goosepimples formed a blanket all over her skin immediately. She couldn't figure out whether it was fear she felt—but something didn't seem at all right. She giggled nervously, not giving it much weight. Miss Bernard opened the door to the classroom. She wanted to tell the students to leave from the doorway but something made her decide against it. She cleared her throat and went in.

Charlie joined his friends outside the door.

Miss Bernard didn't mark any papers. She couldn't. She sat watching the door for the hour or so she had left, wondering why she felt so nervous, afraid. When the clock on her desk signalled

the end of detention, she stood up and addressed the students;
"Okay boys and girls, thanks for being well behaved today. I am happy I do not have to write up any of you for a second session. You can all go now."

There was a huge sigh of relief in the room.

"So, see you tomorrow guys," she added.

"See you tomorrow, Miss," they chorused, some getting up immediately, others packing away their things.

"Now, please behave so Principal Daniels don't sanction us all here again tomorrow."

A chorused but quiet laugh travelled over the room.

Ashley looked back at her, smiled and winked, saying, "Promise to, Miss."

Miss Bernard smiled at her as she disappeared out the door.

The teacher started packing up as soon as the last boy left the room. She looked towards the door and the kids from earlier were still there. She scrutinized them. Something about them didn't seem right. Mrs Bernard felt strange but she couldn't quite put her finger on why.

When she came outside the classroom, the group parted for her to pass. Goosepimples casted a blanket over her skin again, but this time, she felt a chill in the air.

The group watched as she went towards the exit.

The next day, Miss Lynn entered her classroom as usual—all smiles. As Nico took her books from her and carried them over to the desk, Miss Lynn addressed the class, "Good morning, everyone. I hope you have all had a restful night and are ready to take on the day."

"Good morning, Miss Lynn," the class sang.

"We have," a few of them added.

"Very well. Today, we'll be doing a little pop quiz."

"Nooo," said the whole class, discouraged.

"Come on, don't moan." She smiled as she passed between the desks to distribute the papers she'd taken out of her desk drawer. "I made it easy, so you don't even have to try." She smiled as she said this.

She walked back to her desk and checked the time on the small clock sat atop it. She looked up at her class, everyone waiting for her to give her command. "Alright then. You can start. And remember, everyone should work independently. If you have any questions, raise your hand and I will come see to you."

The test began, and the teacher kept a close watch on the class to ensure that no one copied. No one called her to query anything in the test, and soon the thirty minutes was gone—time was up. Miss Lynn called the end of the test and everyone walked up to her desk to hand their papers back.

She carried on with class, finishing up the rest of her lesson. Today's lesson was focussed on Pythagoras' theorem. This was the fourth and final lesson on the topic and Miss Lynn was relived to see that most of her students understood the topic well. She gave them a few problems to solve, allowing students to come up to the board to solve them one by one.

She was just about to move on from the topic when the bell rang. At the ring of the bell, everyone started to rush out of the classroom. "Don't forget to do the exercises on pages 67 through to 72 in the textbook. We will go over the answers on Monday. Remember, the marks will go towards your final grades."

"See you tomorrow, Miss!" some students said.

"Goodbye," she said and smiled at the group of five as they left the room.

They were the last to leave the room and Miss Lynn watched them through the window as they walked by the window. She didn't understand why they stuck together so much. Even in her days, she hadn't witnessed anything like it. Kids joined groups, sure, but they were never so attached to the hip. She scratched her brain but couldn't remember ever seeing one without the other.

In her classroom, Miss Bernard was sitting, waiting for her students to come in. All of a sudden, a cold air passed through her classroom, chilling her to the bones. As if in slow motion, she looked up to find the same group from outside detention yesterday walking by. One of them turned in her direction and their eyes met. Fear washed over her and she tried to shake it off quickly. She looked up again and the group was gone.

Miss Lynn marked a test paper as she waited for her next set of students. "Wrong, right, wrong, wrong... Right. Bravo William, more than 50% this time," she said, placing the boy's test on top of the marked pile. She took the next one up, checking her phone to see how much longer she had. The students were moving between classes now, each having ten minutes before they had to get to their next class. She had four more minutes, enough to mark another paper.

She was marking the paper when she realised she'd seen those exact same answers before. Miss Lynn was sure she wasn't mistaking it. She went through the small pile of marked papers and found the one she was looking for.

Confusion washed over her. She watched them the whole time; they did not copy from each other. She was sure. How did they write down the exact same answers word for word? She was confused but determined to find out what was going on; how this happened without her noticing.

Could it be? I have to check, she thought. As she picked up the pile of unmarked papers, the students started filing in. She would have to wait until later to see whether she was right.

Miss Lynn declined to sit with Mrs McKinley at lunch. She set her water bottle on the desk and retrieved the set of test papers from her desk drawer. She searched through them, finding the set she was looking for.

"What in the world is going on here?" she exclaimed. Every one of the five students answered the same questions using the same responses in the same order. There was no differentiation whatsoever. They all got the same questions incorrect for the same reason. Their papers were identical. It was as if one person wrote all five papers but the handwritings were not the same. It was obvious they each wrote their own paper.

She found it very strange and became even more suspicious. This was disturbing for Miss Lynn. She replayed the test session in her head. What did she miss?

The day continued and Miss Lynn carried on as necessary. She didn't see the group again for the rest of the day but they were on her mind the whole time. She was going to get to the bottom of this, whatever it was.

The following week, Monday came and Miss Lynn was still baffled. In fact, it had kept her up most of the weekend. She couldn't remember whether this had ever happened before. She wondered who she could talk to without raising any alarms that would get the students into trouble unnecessarily. That worry didn't last long, though, because Miss Bernard came to her classroom at lunchtime.

"Hey, are you busy?"

"I'm never too busy for you. Come in, have a seat," she said, offering her the second chair at her desk. She took her lunch from her lunch bag and placed it upon the desk.

"In the mood?" she offered a box with grapes to Miss Bernard.

"Sure, thanks." She took the box and started eating the grapes. She wasn't sure she was making the right decision, but Miss Bernard knew she needed to talk to someone.

"So," Miss Lynn began, "what's up with you?"

"Hmm, not much..."

Miss Lynn could tell that something was on her mind. "What aren't you saying?"

Miss Bernard set the grapes on the desk and planted her face in her palms. She ruffled her hair as she said, "Can I talk to you about something and it stays just between us?"

"Of course. You know I wouldn't repeat anything you say to me to anyone."

"Yes, but this is not about me, Louise. You have to promise me..." She was almost hyperventilating.

"Brit, I promise. Talk to me." She rested her hand on her friend's knee. Miss Bernard was red in the face. "Hey, talk to me."

"I don't know... I don't exactly know what is going on but I know something isn't right."

"Okay, let's try to figure it out together. First, tell me what you're talking about."

Miss Bernard looked at her, wondering if she had made the right decision.

"Bernie—" the two teachers laughed. Miss Lynn knew that would do the trick. She hated to be called that.

"Okay," Miss Bernard began. "The thing is, there is this group of kids..."

Miss Lynn sat up straight at that. "Yeah?"

"I don't know what it is but something about them unsettles me. Whenever they are near—I don't have to see them, it's like my whole body senses them—I become... I don't know if scared is the right term."

Miss Lynn was waiting to hear what she suspected now. She pushed her sandwich over and rested her elbow on the desk, resting her chin on her folded knuckles.

"It's like they aren't human or something. Oh no," she covered her mouth with both hands. "I shouldn't say that. I don't know them like that but... I've said too much—"

"You haven't. But let me get this straight, you think something is up with them." She nodded her head, yes. "Do you mind saying who they are?" Miss Lynn knew exactly who she was speaking about but didn't want to give too much away. She was sure she'd look into them now. Without a doubt.

"That group that Charlie Henley is a part of. You know those five... They..."

"I think I know who you are talking about."

"You do? Don't they creep you out?"

"I can't say they do but that doesn't mean that your feelings aren't valid. Tell you what; I'll look into it to see if there is something off with them then I can contribute a bit more to the conversation."

"Thanks so much, Louise. You have no idea what this means to me. I haven't slept in days. It's like they occupy my mind completely."

Miss Bernard was shaking. Miss Lynn patted her friend on the knee, "Come here, let me give you a hug," she said, standing up. The two embraced each other, Miss Bernard feeling relieved.

"I can't thank you enough for this. I hope it's nothing. Surely, they can't be bad kids. Maybe I'm just feeling off."

"Let's hope they aren't. We'll get to the bottom of this regardless."

The friends sat and had lunch together, with Miss Bernard not eating much. She barely picked at her food. When the bell rang, they said their goodbyes and Miss Bernard returned to her classroom, although reluctantly.

Though Miss Lynn didn't share her concerns with Miss Bernard, there was no way she wasn't going to get to the bottom of what was going on. She too was suspicious of this group and this new information gave her even more reasons to be. It all seemed too strange to her. She got to work. All week, she followed them and went through as much of their records as she could. She was beginning to piece things together and the more she found out, the more confused she became.

Firstly, when it came to extramural activities, they all chose football. Miss Lynn went to a couple of the practices and she noticed that two of the boys were good at the sport, while the other two weren't by any means even close to good. The only girl of their group was the fastest on the field but only chased her opponents around on the field. She wasn't good with the ball at all. *Why do those three play football if they can't? Wouldn't it be better to play something simpler like tennis or volleyball?* she thought to herself as she watched them.

She made a note of this in a notebook.

It didn't take long for Miss Lynn to think that she was overthinking everything. She even tried convincing herself that she was making everything up in her head and went back to the test papers quite a few times to see if she would see something different. To think something was up with these kids was too much for her to bear. They were kids after all.

At the cafeteria, she observed them once more. She stood just to the side of where the food was being served and she waited for the group. When she finally saw them come into the cafeteria together as expected, she paid close attention to them.

They lined up right behind each other, one after the other. Another student even tried to break their group, which they didn't allow. Even more strange was the fact that whatever food was taken by the first in the group was also taken by all the others. First the bread, then the salad, pasta, and finally the dessert. There was a wide variety. Their cafeteria was always praised for their lunch menu in both variations and taste. But the group took all the same thing. Most friends group would have taken different things so that they could share. *Strange,* she thought.

The teacher made a mental note of this, she would write it down later. Miss Lynn was suspicious, but part of her still felt like she was just imagining things. She kept telling herself that they were all just a close group of friends.

When the five of them all went to sit at the same table, the teacher did not take her eyes off them. There, she saw something that surprised her the most. As if to confirm her suspicion, the five of them ate at the same time. Not like a group of people sitting down to eat at dinner time. No, they ate like they were doing some form of synchronized eating routine. They each took a bite, chewed, and when everyone was done, they took another. They almost looked like machines; this caused a shiver to go up the teacher's back.

Now she was nervous.

She kept staring at them and this was the first time that she noticed that they all had on the exact same outfit.

How did I not notice that before? Someone bumped into her and she apologised without taking her eyes off the group.

She noted what they were wearing: black t-shirts, denim pants, open green jackets, a chain bracelet on the left wrist each, and black eyeshadow.

"What?" she said a little too loud, causing the students close to her to look at her.

"Miss?" one student asked.

"No, nothing. Carry on."

The students did just that.

Miss Lynn stood there baffled, unable to believe her own eyes. She continued to watch them, eventually following them back to their class. And yes, they seemed to take all the same classes.

At the end of the week, Miss Lynn complied all of her findings on her laptop. She found herself engaged in a conversation with herself as she collated everything she'd found.

"Why do these kids look so strange? Surely, there is something unusual about them; they seem almost...unnatural." She was shocked at her words. "No, I can't think these things about my students, no matter who they are. It's true, they are a bit strange, but I certainly can't start ridiculing them. Aah, I can already see my butt sitting on the chair in front of the principal; he'll fire me for discrimination."

The math teacher was frightened of the consequences of discovering the true nature of her students.

"Maybe I should collect more evidence, but really, on what basis; that they are strange?!" She pushed away her laptop and slammed her fist on her desk. She started hyperventilating, covered her face, and screamed in her hands, "What have I gotten myself into here? I can't do this. I don't care what they are. They don't bother me. But they scare Brit and I understand why. No, I have to do something. I have to get to the bottom of this. No, I can. I shouldn't. They are kids!"

Now she was having a mental breakdown.

"No! I have to figure this out. Something isn't right and I have to get to the bottom of it!" she said more determined than ever.

The next few days passed with her worrying about how to do things without affecting her job or the kids, just in case she was wrong about them. It was Monday again and time for another week of school. Miss Lynn entered the classroom again with a lot of papers in her hand. "Well class, today's a pop quiz!"

"No! Again?" someone yelled.

"It's for your own good. I have to prepare you for the final exam of the semester," she said, but it was more an excuse.

At the end of the test, after all the students left, she took only the tests of the five students and compared them all.

For the first answer all the boxes were filled with A, the second all D, the third to fifth were marked B-A-C, respectively. The sixth, which was an open ended question, was answered in the exact same way with the exact same words. "Ooh, I was right!" she said as if she had made a significant discovery. She checked her own definition of perpendicular lines. Her definition did not match theirs. She almost shouted internally.

"Their answer is correct but that's not the way I defined it. How did they do it, though?" She sat back in her chair thinking for a while.

"Okay, maybe... Uh... I don't know... If I show these to the principal, he will surely do something. What would I say—that I didn't see them copying but they cheater?"

She thought some more then eventually decided to go to Mr Daniels' office. When she walked past Miss Bernard's classroom and saw that she still wasn't back at school, it hastened her steps. Miss Bernard had taken off school the week before and wasn't even answering her calls. The last few days she'd seen her, she didn't look like herself anymore and she'd told her that she wasn't coping anymore. She felt like this kids were taunting her.

"This is your responsibility, Miss Lynn," Mr Daniels said, averting her responsibilities.

Miss Lynn was appalled by his words. "What?"

The principal pointed to the tests, and with a very serious look, said, "It's the responsibility of a teacher to make sure that the pupils don't copy from each other, so this is a matter for you to resolve. If you can't even prevent five students from copying from each other, then it means you're not a good teacher at all," he scoffed.

"B-But... Principal Daniels, those kids don't even sit close to each other, and then look at the writing! They are all identical, as if only one person wrote all of them!"

"This is even worse. This means that you haven't even noticed that tests are being exchanged. Miss, this upsets me, and I think I will have to add this to your file. Thanks for bringing it to my attention," he said the last sentence with so much sarcasm.

"What?! Are you saying this is my fault? I am trying to bring your attention to something serious here. Something is wrong," Miss Lynn said, shocked.

"All I have seen here is that you have a few students who may or may not have cheated on a class test because you as the teacher weren't paying attention to them. And what exactly is wrong that I have to look into? I have to worry about running this school as well as do your job too? I expected better from you, Miss Lynn. I have always thought of you as one of my best teachers. And whatever it is that you want me to investigate, bring me some evidence. Otherwise, I will have to suspend you because you're unsuitable for the job."

"I am a great teacher. And all I am saying is that these students are weird." She almost kicked herself when the words left her lips. She screamed at herself inside.

"Mind your words, Miss Lynn, or I'll have to fire you on the spot for discrimination!" Principal Daniels shouted, standing up behind his desk. Being bullied when he was growing up made him intolerant to name calling. He wouldn't stand for it.

Miss Lynn, frightened by these words, did not say anything else. She wanted to apologise but she couldn't risk making him angrier.

The principal sighed, then sat down again. "Now, go. I'm a very busy man. But let me warn you, if you continue with this nonsense, you will force my hand."

The teacher clenched her fists in anger, then she got up and walked away.

Outside the principal's office, she realized that she couldn't do anything more. Maybe she was a bit naïve going to him with the little she had. She had to let it go. She would always be the one in the wrong, no matter what she did, because they were minors and she was an adult. Besides, what exactly did she have on them? All she had was a few kids who did things in a different way.

But they scare the daylights out of my friend and now she's not even at school anymore. She loves this job more than anything else and they are pushing away from it.

This made her very angry, and in that moment of anger, she went to look for them.

After searching for some time, she found them in an empty classroom. They were gathered in a circle and seemed to be talking softly to each other. Miss Lynn, impatient and angry, puffed out her chest in anger and went in to confront them.

"You!" she said, attracting the attention of the group. "Who are you? Why are you so in tune with each other? Why are you all so attached to each other? Do any of you know how to exists on your own?" Anger boiled inside her.

The five of them stared at her in silence then, after a moment, they answered, finishing each other's sentences. "You teacher..."

"You're an annoying person..."

"Nosy even.

"And we don't like nosy people..."

"For this, we always make them disappear."

These words drove fear inside her instantly. "Make them... disappear?" she repeated.

Suddenly, the pupils of the five became vertical all at once and their eyes went almost black.

"Wh-what... What are you? You're not humans!" She wanted to run but found that she couldn't move.

Together the students laughed menacingly.

"You're right," one of them began.

"We're not humans," another one added.

"We're vampires," they said in unison.

"V-Vampires?!" Miss Lynn couldn't believe her ears. "But you can go out in the daylight. I saw you eating garlic bread... How can you if you're vampires?"

"Why does everyone always ask those stupid questions? You know nothing about vampires."

"All those stupid things you humans believe does not apply to us."

"We are strong."

"We all feed from a single source."

"This is why we are so strong and ALWAYS... What would you call it..."

"United?"

"Nope. In sync."

Miss Lynn trembled. They were driving the fear of god in her. She was so scared that she cried and shivered, all without moving from the spot where she stood.

The five circled the woman very slowly. As they moved closer to her, she trembled even more. When she felt their breaths on her, she wet herself. Her jaw trembled and her teeth clashed against each other. Without warning, they sank their teeth into several parts of her all at the same time. The woman lost all the blood in her body within seconds. She was dead. They stepped away and her body fell to the ground in one smooth motion.

"Excuse us, Miss, we wouldn't have touched you if you hadn't meddled," they said in unison.

Since the five students started high school in the city a few months ago, many houses had been left empty. Some still had clothes hanging in the garden, the grass hadn't been cut for what seemed like centuries, and the homes hadn't been cleaned in months. These houses all had one thing in common. They were in rather shabby states now.

They looked like ghost houses, once inhabited and then empty. As if its inhabitants had just disappeared overnight, and so was Miss Bernard's house since last week.